The Bravest of the Brave

The Bravest of the Brave

by **Shutta Crum** • illustrated by **Tim Bowers**

Alfred A. Knopf ⫶ New York

THIS IS A BORZOI BOOK PUBLISHED BY ALFRED A. KNOPF

Text copyright © 2005 by Shutta Crum

Illustrations copyright © 2005 by Tim Bowers

All rights reserved under International and Pan-American Copyright Conventions. Published in
the United States by Alfred A. Knopf, an imprint of Random House Children's Books, a division
of Random House, Inc., New York, and simultaneously in Canada by Random House of Canada
Limited, Toronto. Distributed by Random House, Inc., New York.

www.randomhouse.com/kids

Library of Congress Cataloging-in-Publication Data

Crum, Shutta.
The bravest of the brave / by Shutta Crum ; illustrated by Tim Bowers. — 1st ed.
p. cm.
SUMMARY: A fearless little skunk sets off through the woods alone at night encountering scary
creatures, which the reader can correctly identify as various forest animals.
ISBN 0-375-82637-8 (trade) — ISBN 0-375-92637-2 (lib. bdg.)
[1. Skunks—Fiction. 2. Courage—Fiction. 3. Night—Fiction. 4. Forest animals—Fiction.
5. Forests and forestry—Fiction. 6. Stories in rhyme.] I. Bowers, Tim, ill. II. Title.
PZ8.3.C88643Br 2005
[E]—dc22
2004011045

MANUFACTURED IN CHINA
January 2005
10 9 8 7 6 5 4 3 2 1
First Edition

To my colleagues at the Ann Arbor District Library—
who are all resourceful and brave. Working with you
has been one of the great joys of my life.
—S.C.

Remembering sweet baby Sarah Gray
—T.B.

Late one day I hurried home,

Stepping through the wood alone.

It was **deep** and **DIM**; I could barely see.

But I thought **brave** thoughts to comfort me.

Then . . .

In the shadows, quietly,

1 masked face stared right at me!

So I *sang* my song as SURELY as I could

And off raced the robber through the

deep *dark* wood.

Then . . .

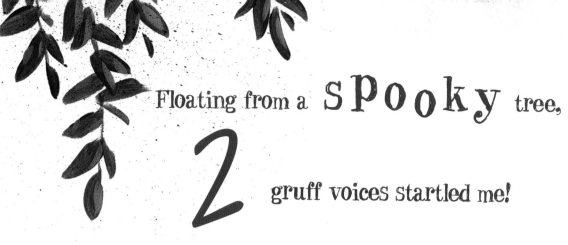

Floating from a SPOOky tree,

2 gruff voices startled me!

So I ruffed my fur as FULLY as I could

And away howled ghosts through the

deep dark wood.

Then . . .

Slipping low, so silently,

3 silk nets dropped over me!

So I **danced** my dance as **wildly** as I could

And back tramped   the trappers through the

deep dark wood.

Then . . .

Pricking hard and angrily,

4 long fingers poked at me!

So I **stomped** my stomp as **LOUDLY** as I could

And away scurried witches through the

deep dark wood.

Then . . .

Mother!

Spying down, quite fearsomely,

5 sharp faces scowled at me!

So I *called* my call as CLEARLY as I could

And off sailed the pirates through the

deep dark wood.

Then . . .

From the darkness, suddenly,

6 STRONG arms

all groped for me!

So I made a stance as

STOUTLY as I could.

And . . .

I pawed the ground as

GRAVELY as I could.

And . . .

I raised . . .

my tail as MOTHER

said I should!

When . . .

squinting hard so I could see—

There they were, my family!

So they brought me HOME as quickly as they could,

Right here to our party in the

deep dark wood.

Then . . .

Telling tales of bravery,

7 times they heard from me!

For I stood up TALL, as **boldly** as I could,

And I scared all my friends in the

deep dark wood.

Oh, my! Then . . .

Flashing round so cheerily,

8 bright lights encircled me!

So I **laughed** out loud as $g\,a\,i\,l\,y$ as I could

And we lit the night up in the

deep *dark* wood.

Then . . .

Snuggled close by family,

9 big hugs they gave to me!

So they T U C K E D me in as *gently* as they could

And I nestled safely in my **deep dark** wood.

S h h - h - h . . .

Way up high, the sky is deep.

10 stars twinkle while I sleep.

They are keeping watch, beaming peacefully,

For the BRAVEST of the *BRAVE*, and . . . that is me!